# Thumbelina
# Thinks Big!

by Katie Dale

and Rupert Van Wyk

# W
# FRANKLIN WATTS
LONDON•SYDNEY

This story is based on the traditional fairy tale,
*Thumbelina* but with a new twist.
You can read the original story in
Hopscotch Fairy Tales. Can you make
up your own twist for the story?

Franklin Watts
First published in Great Britain in 2015 by The Watts Publishing Group

Text © Katie Dale 2015
Illustrations © Rupert Van Wyk 2015

The rights of Katie Dale to be identified as the author
and Rupert Van Wyk as the illustrator of this Work have been asserted
in accordance with the Copyright, Designs and Patents Act, 1988.

ISBN 978 1 4451 4295 1 (hbk)
ISBN 978 1 4451 4296 8 (pbk)
ISBN 978 1 4451 4298 2 (library ebook)

Series Editor: Melanie Palmer
Series Advisor: Catherine Glavina
Series Designer: Peter Scoulding
Cover Designer: Cathryn Gilbert

Printed in China

Franklin Watts
An imprint of
Hachette Children's Group
Part of The Watts Publishing Group
Carmelite House
50 Victoria Embankment
London EC4Y 0DZ

An Hachette UK Company
www.hachette.co.uk

www.franklinwatts.co.uk

MIX
Paper from
responsible sources
FSC® C104740
www.fsc.org

Once there was an old couple
who were desperate for a child.

They were wonderful babysitters, made up fantastic stories for the village children – and even did all the voices!

5

But every night they went back to
their empty home and wished on
the evening star:
"Starlight, star bright, please
bring us a child tonight."

One night a fairy heard their wish,
and smiled. "They would make
wonderful parents," she said.
So she planted a seed outside
their window.

The seed grew and, to the couple's surprise, inside the flower was a tiny girl!

"Why, you're no bigger than my thumb!" the woman smiled. "We'll call you Thumbelina."

Thumbelina was so small she found lots of things a bit tricky. Playing sports ...

eating out ...

even walking along the street!

But she was very good at dressmaking. She had to be – normal clothes didn't fit her!

One day, a fashion show came to town. "What beautiful clothes!" Thumbelina cried. "I wish I could be a model!"

Her friends laughed. "Models are tall, Thumbelina, and you are very small – you can't be a model!"

Thumbelina frowned.

"Don't listen, Thumbelina," said her parents. "Wishes can come true. You can do anything if you try hard enough."

All night long, Thumbelina stitched and stuck and glued and glittered, until she had made her best dress ever – a dress fit for a fashion show! "Now they'll notice me!" she smiled.

The next day, Thumbelina sneaked backstage. She was so small, no one even saw her! She tiptoed past the dressing room ... past the other models ...

Finally she climbed up onto the catwalk. This was her big chance! Excitedly, she stepped out into the spotlight ...

But nobody saw her except
a little girl. "Mummy, look!"
the girl cried. "Someone's
dropped their doll!"

"I'm not a doll!" Thumbelina shouted crossly. "I'm a model! Look at my beautiful dress!"

"It's amazing!" said the girl's mum.

"I've never seen anything like it! My, the stitching's so neat and tiny I can barely even see it. Who made such a wonderful thing?"

Thumbelina smiled. "I did."

"You're a very talented fashion designer," the woman said. "Would you like to work for me, making clothes and modelling them too?"

Thumbelina beamed.

"You want me to be a model?
Aren't I too small?"

"Not for my clothes," smiled the woman.

So Thumbelina's wish came true, and soon she became famous for designing and modelling the most beautiful clothes …

... for dolls!

# Puzzle 1

Put these pictures in the correct order.
Which event do you think is most important?
Now try writing the story in your own words!

# Puzzle 2

Choose the correct speech bubbles for each character. Can you think of any others? Turn over to find the answers.

# Answers

## Puzzle 1

The correct order is: 1e, 2f, 3d, 4a, 5c, 6b

## Puzzle 2

Thumbelina: 1, 4

The old couple: 2, 6

The fashion designer: 3, 5

## Look out for more Hopscotch Twisty Tales and Must Know Stories:

**TWISTY TALES**

The Lovely Duckling
ISBN 978 1 4451 1633 4

Hansel and Gretel
and the Green Witch
ISBN 978 1 4451 1634 1

The Emperor's New Kit
ISBN 978 1 4451 1635 8

Rapunzel and the
Prince of Pop
ISBN 978 1 4451 1636 5

Dick Whittington
Gets on his Bike
ISBN 978 1 4451 1637 2

The Pied Piper and
the Wrong Song
ISBN 978 1 4451 1638 9

The Princess and the
Frozen Peas
ISBN 978 1 4451 0675 5

Snow White Sees the Light
ISBN 978 1 4451 0676 2

The Elves and the Trendy
Shoes
ISBN 978 1 4451 0678 6

The Three Frilly Goats Fluff
ISBN 978 1 4451 0677 9

Princess Frog
ISBN 978 1 4451 0679 3

Rumpled Stilton Skin
ISBN 978 1 4451 0680 9

Jack and the Bean Pie
ISBN 978 1 4451 0182 8

Brownilocks and the Three
Bowls of Cornflakes
ISBN 978 1 4451 0183 5

Cinderella's Big Foot
ISBN 978 1 4451 0184 2

Little Bad Riding Hood
ISBN 978 1 4451 0185 9

Sleeping Beauty –
100 Years Later
ISBN 978 1 4451 0186 6

**MUST KNOW STORIES
LEVEL1:**

The Gingerbread Man
ISBN 978 1 4451 2819 1*
ISBN  978 1 4451 2820 7

The Three Little Pigs
ISBN 978 14451 2823 8*
ISBN 978 14451 2824 5

Jack and the Beanstalk
ISBN 978 14451 2827 6*
ISBN 978 14451 2828 3

The Boy Who Cried Wolf
ISBN 978 14451 2831 3*
ISBN 978 14451 2832 0

The Three Billy Goats Gruff
ISBN 978 14451 2835 1*
ISBN 978 14451 2836 8

The Three Billy Goats Gruff
ISBN 978 14451 2835 1*
ISBN 978 14451 2836 8

Little Red Riding Hood
ISBN 978 14451 2839 9*
ISBN 978 14451 2840 5

Goldilocks and the
Three Bears
ISBN 978 14451 2843 6 *
ISBN 978 14451 2844 3

Hansel and Gretel
ISBN 978 14451 2847 4*
ISBN 978 14451 2848 1

The Little Red Hen
ISBN 978 14451 2851 1*
ISBN 978 14451 2852 8

Dick Whittington
ISBN 978 14451 2855 9*
ISBN 978 14451 2856 6

Rapunzel
ISBN 978 14451 2859 7*
ISBN 978 14451 2860 3

*hardback

**For more Hopscotch books go to:**
www.franklinwatts.co.uk